# With a Whoop and a Holler

## A BUSHEL OF LORE FROM WAY DOWN SOUTH

by **NANCY VAN LAAN**    illustrated by **SCOTT COOK**

AN ANNE SCHWARTZ BOOK
Atheneum Books for Young Readers

For my dear ol' Ma, whose deep Southern ties have given me a lifetime of warm
recollections and a persistent hankering for black-eyed peas —N. V. L.

For Granny, who loves to laugh, loves to tell a good story, and at 97 still loves
to plant her butter beans each spring —S. C.

ACKNOWLEDGMENTS
Many thanks to Linda Goss, cofounder of the National Festival of Black Storytelling
for her review of the manuscript; to my trusting editor, Anne Schwartz, for her constant support
and encouragement from beginning to end; and to Sauveur Dorcilien of New York City
for his help in the translation of Creole words and expressions. —N. V. L.

With much appreciation to Anne Schwartz, Ann Bobco, Sarah Knight, and Ed Miller.
And to my family and friends for their help and encouragement. —S. C.

Atheneum Books for Young Readers
An imprint of Simon & Schuster Children's Publishing Division
1230 Avenue of the Americas
New York, New York 10020
Text copyright © 1998 by Nancy Van Laan
Illustrations copyright © 1998 by Scott Cook
All rights reserved including the right of reproduction in whole or in part in any form.
Book design by Edward Miller
The text of this book is set in Clearface.
The illustrations are rendered in mixed medium,
using watercolor, gouache, pastel, and acrylics.
First Edition
Printed in Hong Kong
10 9 8 7 6 5 4 3
Library of Congress Cataloging-in-Publication Data
Van Laan, Nancy.
With a whoop and a holler : a bushel of lore from way down south /
retold by Nancy Van Laan ; illustrated by Scott Cook.—1st ed.
p. cm.
"An Anne Schwartz book."
Summary: A collection of tales, rhymes, riddles, superstitions, and sayings organized around the
three distinct regions of the South: the Bayou, the Deep South, and Appalachia.
ISBN 0-689-81061-X
1. Tales—Southern States. [1. Folklore—Southern States.] I. Cook, Scott, ill. II. Title.
PZ8.1.V4524Wi  1998
398'.0975—dc20 [E]
96-24336

# Table of contents

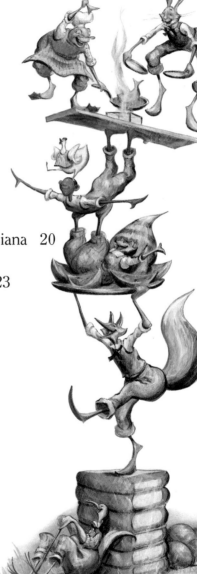

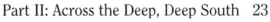

# Introduction

Those of us with a finely tuned ear can often identify which part of the United States someone hails from by listening to their accent. But almost anybody can tell right off if that person is from down South.

Saying "y'all" for "you" is the mark of a true Southerner. Answering "ma'am" or "sir" when spoken to by an elder is another dead giveaway. But the real clincher is that melodious Southern drawl. Words pour out so soft and thick, they make you feel all warm and cozy, like you're resting on a feather bed with a hand-me-down quilt. Have you ever been asked to "take a load off your feet" and "lazy awhile"? Or have you been invited to "chaw the fat" or told to "looky yonder"? Have you tasted food that's "dish-lickin' good," or gone "bandadooin' about"? Down South, there are enough made-up words and expressions to fill the pages of a good-sized dictionary.

There's lots else that makes the South stand apart from the rest of the country. More than other places, life seems to move at a slower pace. This is most apparent in the summertime, when the sizzling sun is hot enough to fry an egg on the sidewalk and the humidity makes your clothes stick to your skin like cotton candy. Porch sitting, still considered an occupation of the highest order, fulfills the need to rest or to greet whoever passes by with a nod of the head and a "how-da-doo."

But what the South is really famous for is its "down-home cookin'." Every so often, I find a reason to return to Alabama just so I can "pig out" on fried chicken, pork barbecue, grits, gravy, black-eyed peas, turnip greens, corn bread, biscuits, and pecan pie—all of it in one sitting!

"Dropping in" is also typical in the South. My grandmother's home was always full of drop-ins. Nanny would say, "Why don't you set for a spell?" and everybody did. Lots of times the visits would last a whole afternoon or until late in the evening. Uncles, aunts, and cousins would wander in, and so would the neighbors, and not one of them would leave until they had "had their say." We'd laugh our "fool heads" off, listening to all the stories each and everybody told. Every time one person told a story, it reminded somebody else of another, and on and on the telling went, each one trying to outdo the other.

I've never met anyone down South who could not tell a good story. Some of them arise out of personal experiences, some from a juicy tidbit heard told somewhere else. But the teller always tells it as though it had happened to her or him. This makes each story sound like it's being told for the first time.

And each story is treated as though it is a living thing. The teller packs it full of emotion and sometimes jumps off the chair and acts it out, turning it into a performance of high drama. No matter what the subject is, a Southerner will tell it with complete sincerity and conviction. In this way, the story demands to be believed and to be thought of as real—at least, while it is told!

One other thing: No story is ever told twice the same way; why, sometimes there are literally hundreds of versions. So keep this in mind when you read the stories collected here—you probably won't find them told exactly this way anywhere else.

What I've tried to do in *With a Whoop and a Holler* is to make each story as funny as it could possibly be. If this meant trimming a bit by snipping out a thing or two, or stretching certain parts to extend the humor, then that's what I did. At the same time, I used all the words and expressions I could conjure out of my own experiences growing up among a bunch of fun-loving Southern folks who didn't know the meaning of telling it like it was. So feel free to retell these stories in your own words if you like— and have a good time doing it.

This collection is organized around the three distinct regions of the South—the Bayou, the Deep South, and the Mountains—because each has its own unique way of saying things. Though all are distinctly Southern, each is full of enough peculiarities to draw attention to itself. In the stories from the bayous and mountains, I have retained most of the original dialect. However, I replaced the plantation English—the so-called Negro dialect recorded over a hundred years ago in the stories from the Deep South— with the more familiar Southern talk I grew up with.

I chose stories I loved, which also happen to be the ones I felt most comfortable retelling. Whenever possible, I picked those not found in other collections for children, but of course, a couple of Uncle Remus stories and at least one Jack tale had to be included, for these are so universally identified with Southern folk literature as a whole. The rhymes, riddles, and superstitions were tossed in here and there to add a little seasoning to the stew.

Keep in mind that some tales—like those of Brer Rabbit, for instance—are so familiar, it would be hard to pinpoint exactly where in the South they were first heard. This holds true for the rhymes, riddles, superstitions, and sayings as well. Just because a folklorist may have first heard a certain riddle in North Carolina doesn't mean it wasn't told somewhere else, too.

As you sit back and listen to or tell the stories in this collection, try to picture the South in your mind. Begin in Louisiana, where you can pole your way through the thick, misty waters of the bayous that weave through marshland like an endless maze. Then let your mind wander down to the lowlands of the Carolinas and Georgia, full of cypress swamps and sandy soil, where alligators hunt and herons fly and moss hangs heavy on the water oaks. Wander over and smell the pines on the hills of northern Georgia and Alabama in the springtime, and feel the deep-orange clay soil covered with flowering dogwoods, sweet-smelling honeysuckle, and dark, shining magnolia leaves, full of scented white blossoms. Finally, head up to the Blue Ridge Mountains or the Great Smokies, snow-covered in winter, where valleys are filled with a soft, blue haze. And take yourself way back to that long-ago time when animals and people talked and acted "right foolish" on occasion—just like some folks do today!

—N. V. L.

# The United States

WASHINGTON

MONTANA

NORTH DAKOTA

OREGON

IDAHO

SOUTH DAKOTA

WYOMING

NEBRASKA

Pacific
Ocean

NEVADA

UTAH

COLORADO

KANSAS

CALIFORNIA

OKLAHO

ARIZONA

NEW MEXICO

TEXAS

# PART I
# Down in the Bayou

Louisiana is patterned like a patchwork quilt, with the watery threads of the giant Mississippi weaving southward, constantly shifting and remapping the landscape. As it winds through pine-covered hills to the lowlands, the mighty river widens. Its branches become slow-moving waters called bayous, or they form huge swamps and saltwater marshes before emptying into the Gulf. Though water shapes the land, it's the people of Louisiana, with their variety of unique cultures, that give this state its vibrant color.

Long ago, the Caddo and other native groups lived all over this region. Then the Spanish came, and soon after, the French. The Caddo now live on a reservation in Oklahoma, where their stories are kept alive. One of these, a sly trickster tale called "Possum Plays Dead," is every bit as funny as any Brer Rabbit story told down South.

Nowadays, it's the French Creole and Cajun cultures that set Louisiana apart from the rest of the country. Creoles are descendants of the early French and Spanish settlers. Cajuns, also known as Acadians, migrated from French Canada during the late 1700s. Both groups created their own patois, a combination of French and other languages blended into one. Today their patois are not spoken nearly as much as they once were, but they can still be heard in songs and stories.

Originally the Creole and Cajun people did not mingle much, for they lived in different parts of the state. The Creoles stayed near the Gulf or in the big cities of New Orleans and Baton Rouge, while the Cajuns staked out farmland further inland and built their homes along the bayous, great places to fish and hunt.

Even so, they still have a lot in common. Both are known for their spicy stew called gumbo and a lot of other dishes found nowhere else. Each also has its own brand of music, underscored with lively singing and dancing. And best of all, both brought along an endless supply of funny stories when they arrived in Louisiana—and both keep on telling them!

The Creoles and Cajuns also use proverbs (old sayings) to emphasize points they're trying to make in the course of conversations. They have the right saying for just about any situation. Some of my favorites are included in this book.

A blending of African-American culture with the Creole produced clever tales like "Monkey Stew." The African-American Creoles also tell stories about Brer Rabbit, but as you will see in "One Cold Day," their wise rabbit speaks French and goes by the name of Compé Lapin.

The Cajuns have a different bunch of tales, about a "noodlehead," or a stupid person, called Fool John. These stories came with them from Canada and are similar to the old English folktales about a boy named Foolish Jack.

As you read or are told these Bayou tales, listen to the distinctive rhythm—unlike the soft, melodious, and rambling accounts so often heard in the Southern lowlands or the long, drawn-out verse of the mountain folk. Spun with a French twist, they are direct and to the point, told in a matter-of-fact, offhand way. But that doesn't mean they aren't filled with hilarious goings-on!

# Dreamland

Dreamland opens here;
Sweep the dream path clear!
Listen, chile, dear little chile,
To the song of the crocodile.

3

# Glossary

bien–good
compé–godfather
là–there
lapin–rabbit
monsieur–mister
oui–yes

# One cold Day

*BRRRR . . . UH!* Eléphant, he is cold, cold, cold!

So Eléphant, he goes off, *trampf, trampf, trampf,* through the snow.

"*BRRRR . . . UH!* I must find a place that is warm," he says.

The next thing you know, Eléphant hears *SSSSSSSSSSSSS!* "Là," he says, "I wonder what that is."

*SSSSSSSSSSSSSSSS!* The noise gets louder.

Eléphant, he stops. He looks down.

What does he see? Nothing but a log lying there.

But then he hears, "Oh, Monsieur Eléphant!"

Eléphant, he thinks that log is talking. He bends down, and his big round ears go *PFHHIT!* They are wide open now, listening.

Then he hears, "I'm so cold, cold, cold! You must help me!"

Eléphant, he looks closer.

It is not a talking log. It is a snake! *HAH!*

So Eléphant, he says, "What is wrong with you?"

"I'm stuck," says Snake. "I crawled under this log to get warm. Now I can't get out."

"I will help you," says Eléphant. Then he lifts up the log with his strong trunk. "Now you can go on."

"*SSSSSSS!* You're no help at all," says Snake, crawling free. "I'm still freezing to death!"

"I will warm you," says Eléphant. "Wrap yourself around my leg."

Snake does so.

Eléphant, he walks along, *tromp, tromp,* with Snake wrapped about his leg.

*SSSSS SSSSS tromp tromp SSSSS SSSSS tromp tromp.*

As Eléphant walks, Snake warms up.

Now Snake unwinds, *urrrrh.* And now he crawls, *SSSSSS,* on top of Eléphant.

So Eléphant, he says, "What is the matter with you?"

"I want to get down, Monsieur Eléphant. But first I want to bite you."

"You want to bite me?"

"I do."

"But why would you want to bite me? I helped you."

"I am a snake. That is what snakes do."

"Snakes do that?"

"Yesssssss."

So Eléphant, he says, "Ah, well, let us go ask Compé Lapin. If he says you should bite me, then I will let you."

Off they go, *tromp tromp SSSS SSSS tromp tromp SSSS SSSS.*

They find Compé Lapin sitting on a stump.

"Ah, Compé Lapin," says Eléphant. "Listen to me. I need your advice." So Eléphant, he tells the whole story.

Then Compé Lapin, he says, "This snake here, he wants to bite you?"

"Ah, oui," says Eléphant.

"Show me where you first met."

*Tromp tromp SSSS SSSS thump thump.* They return to the log.

"Right here, Compé Lapin. Snake was stuck."

"You say he was stuck?"

"Oui, under this log," says Eléphant.

"Ah," says Compé Lapin. "Show me."

Eléphant lifts up the log. Snake crawls under. Eléphant places the log on top of Snake.

Eléphant, he says, "Like so."

"Ah," says Compé Lapin. "Are you sure?"

"Oui, I'm sure," says Eléphant.

Compé Lapin asks Snake, "Is this how it was?"

"Oui," says Snake. "This is just how it was."

"Are you stuck good and tight?"

"Oui," says Snake. "Good and tight."

"Ah bien," says Compé Lapin. "Come, Eléphant, let's go."

So off they went.

And Snake, he stayed just where he was put.

## Tomcat

My father had a big tomcat
That tried to play a fiddle.
He struck it here, he struck it there,
and he struck it in the middle.

## Gumbo

The rooster and the chicken had a fight.
The chicken knocked the rooster out of sight.
The rooster told the chicken, "That's all right—
I'll meet you in the gumbo tomorrow night."

# Glossary

bien—good

bouki—hyena

compé—godfather

l'heure de manger—time to eat

oui—yes

sam-bombel tam—nonsense words

# Monkey Stew

Compé Bouki, he thinks he is so smart, oh yes!

He thinks he shall have a delicious monkey stew for his dinner.

With fire under the kettle and the water oh so hot, Bouki beats his drum and sings,

"Sam-bombel! Sam-bombel tam!

Sam-bombel! Sam-bombel tam!"

When the monkeys, they hear this, they say, "What? Bouki, he has something good to eat! Let's go!"

Bouki is smiling. He hears them come, *swish shwee,* swinging through the trees.

The monkeys, they waste no time at all. They see Bouki, his fine kettle, his strong fire, and sing out, "L'heure de manger, Bouki! Time to eat!"

But Bouki, he says, "Not so fast. First, we play."

"Ah, oui!" say the little monkeys. "We love to play!"

"Watch me," says Bouki. "I will jump into the kettle and when I say I am cooked, pull me out."

"Ah bien! Good!" say the monkeys, and they dance around the kettle, all excited-like.

Bouki, he jumps into the pot of hot water. "Phew! Pull me out quick; I am cooked!"

So the monkeys, they pull Bouki out of the pot.

"Your turn," says Bouki.

So all the monkeys except one, who runs off, jump into the pot of hot water and say, "Phew! Pull us out quick; we are cooked."

Does Bouki do this? Oh, no, no! Instead, he covers the kettle with his blanket.

"If you were cooked," says Bouki, "you could not say so! Heh-heh-heh!"

Now Bouki has a whole kettle of monkeys to eat, except for the one who ran off.

Can you guess what Bouki does the next time he is hungry?

Yes, he lights a fire. Yes, he puts on the kettle. And yes, he sings,

> "Sam-bombel! Sam-bombel tam!
> Sam-bombel! Sam-bombel tam!"

And do the monkeys come? *Oh, yes.*

Does Bouki ask them to play? *Oh, yes.*

Does Bouki jump into the pot? *Oh, yes.*

Does he say, "Pull me out quick; I'm cooked"? *Oh, yes.*

And do they pull him out?

*Ohhhhhhh, no!*

# Tails

The coon's got a long ringed bushy tail;
The possum's tail is bare.
That rabbit ain't got no tail at all,
'Cept a little bunch of hair.

The gobbler's got a big fantail;
The partridge's tail is small.
That peacock's tail's got great big eyes,
But they don't see nothin' at all.

13

# Fool John

One day his ma says to Fool John, she says, "I need a big pot. Go to the neighbor and borrow one."

"Right away, Ma, for sure," says Fool John.

On his way home, Fool John says to himself, "This pot is too big and heavy to carry." So Fool John wears it over his head.

"Where did the sun go?" says Fool John to himself. "I can't see a thing, for sure."

Fool John stumbles and falls down. The pot flies off his head. "Oh, the sun's out again," he says. "Now I can see, for sure."

The pot rolls down the hill to a fork in the road. Fool John picks it up. "Let's have a race," says Fool John to the pot. "You have three legs and I've but two. So you take the long road and I'll take the short road. We'll see who gets home first."

When Fool John gets home, his ma is waiting at the door. "Where's the pot?" she says.

"We had a race," says Fool John, "and, by golly, I won!"

"You fool!" says his ma. "You're the fooliest fool of all. Once more, get out the door! Go back and get the pot."

Again Fool John returns home empty-handed.

"Where's the pot?" asks his ma.

"It's not here, for sure," says Fool John. "It must have run away."

"You fool!" says his ma. "You're the fooliest fool of all. Once more, get out the door! Here's four dollars. Give it to the neighbor for a new pot."

On his way, Fool John hears frogs in the pond singing, "Tite-thwee! Tite-thwee!" He thinks, for sure, they are teasing him.

He holds up his money. "It's four dollars I have—not three!"

The frogs say, "Tite-thwee! Tite-thwee!"

Fool John throws the four dollars into the pond. "Here," Fool John says. "Count it up for yourself!"

"You fool!" says his ma when he comes back home. "You're the fooliest fool of all. Once more, get out the door! Now I need flour. Go to the neighbor and borrow some flour."

On his way back, Fool John sees a hill of ants.

"Look how excited you are to see the flour," says Fool John. "You must be very hungry." So Fool John empties the sack of flour on the ground.

When Fool John gets back, his ma asks, "Where is the flour?"

"I fed it all to the ants, for sure," says Fool John.

"You fool!" says his ma. "You're the fooliest fool of all. Once

15

more, get out the door! I need some lard. Go to the neighbor and borrow some lard."

On his way back, Fool John sees cracks in the ground. He fills the cracks with the lard.

When Fool John gets back his ma asks, "Where is the lard?"

"The ground was chapped, for sure," says Fool John. "So I greased it."

"You fool!" says his ma. "You're the fooliest fool of all. Once more, get out the door! Go tend the sick cow."

Fool John goes outside. He notices the pretty green moss on their  roof.

If the cow eats that moss, it will get well for sure, he thinks.

Fool John gets wood and builds a ladder. He pushes the cow up to the rooftop.

His ma calls out the window, "Fool John, what is thumping and bumping on my roof?"

"The cow," says Fool John.

"The cow?"

"Yes, it's the cow, Ma, for sure."

"The cow is on the roof?"

"Yes, Ma."

"Why is the cow on the roof, Fool John?"

Before Fool John can tell her, the cow goes *Mooo,* falls through, and lands on top of his ma.

"By golly!" says Fool John. "It's about time we got our milk delivered."

*"You fool!"* says his ma.

"I know," says Fool John. "Don't tell me. I'm the fooliest fool of all, for sure!"

# Possum Plays Dead

Once, not so long ago, Possum saw a farmer on his way home from town. The farmer's old wagon was full of corn, sweet potatoes, greens, grits, and many good things to eat.

"Oho!" said Possum. "I know just what to do!"

Possum laid down in the middle of the road and played dead.

The farmer jumped out. "Possum stew is what I shall have," he said.

Then he picked up Possum, threw him into the back of his wagon, and told his horses, "Giddyup!"

Possum picked up some corn. Threw it off.

Picked up some sweet potatoes. Threw them off.

Picked up some greens. Threw them off.

Picked up a bag of grits. Threw it off.

Then Possum threw himself off, gathered up the food, and ran to the woods to eat it all up.

While Possum was eating, along came Fox.

"Where did you get all that?" asked Fox.

Possum told Fox what he had done.

"Well, friend Possum," said Fox, "I'm very hungry. I will try your trick, too."

Fox hid beside the road. Soon another farmer came along. His wagon was also full of good things to eat.

Fox jumped into the middle of the road and played dead, just like Possum had done.

When the farmer saw Fox lying in the middle of the road, he stopped his wagon and grabbed his ax. "Now my wife can have a fur coat!" he said.

"Uh-oh," said Fox. "I'd rather keep my coat and stay hungry!"

As the farmer raised his ax, Fox jumped up and ran off.

Poor ol' Fox! He had to learn the hard way. Only a possum can act like a possum.

# Superstitions
## And Wise Ol' Sayings From Louisiana

The mosquito wastes his time
when he tries to sting alligator.

If you keep your mouth shut,
you won't catch flies.

Cutting off a mule's ears won't make him a horse.

Daddy Tortoise goes
slow; but he gets
to the goal while
Daddy Deer is asleep.

Bouki makes the gumbo;
but Rabbit eats it.

Don't put all your
eggs in one basket.

If you can't
laugh, you
can't keep a
good friend.

If you think too much, you miss all the steps.

If you spit in the sky, it will
fall in your face.

Don't count all
your chickens
before they hatch.

21

# PART II
# Across the Deep, Deep South

Just where, exactly, is the Deep South anyhow? Depends on who you talk to. Folks from Mississippi, Alabama, or Georgia will tell you that *they are* the Deep South and nobody else has the right to claim it. But the people of the Carolinas will certainly argue that point. For the sake of clarity, the stories in this section were collected long ago from *all* these states.

When anybody from anywhere thinks about the stories told in the Deep South, Brer Rabbit immediately comes to mind. Perhaps the most famous trickster of all time, Brer Rabbit can be found in these pages, trying to outfool Brer Frog in "The Big Dinin'," and sassing Colonel Tiger in "The Watermillion Patch." Whether he acts quick-witted, vain, or like a fool, Brer Rabbit nearly always finds a way around a difficult situation or figures out how to outsmart other folk.

"Brer Rabbit" and many other tales were brought over from Africa by slaves. Such stories came to be known as plantation tales because that is where they were originally told and collected. Back then, tellers would often change the tales to reflect their own terrible situation and add an ending where the little guy outsmarts the bigger folk. Thus Brer Rabbit became a folk hero who beat the odds. He and other characters like him symbolized triumph over despair for all the African Americans who endured incredible hardships prior to their emancipation.

There is a special charm in listening to a tale about animals or birds who act human. The creators of this kind of plantation tale must have realized how much more fun an animal story is to tell than one involving people. Usually such stories have a moral, whether it's about somebody who acts too proud, like the bossy rooster in "Ol' Mister Biggety," or too fussy, as the turtle does in "Mister Grumpy Rides the Clouds." "How Come Ol' Buzzard Boards" is an example of another type of tale told here. It's a *chant-fable,* a story that combines song verse with prose. And the little rhymes I've put at the end of each story were used whenever plantation folktales were told.

The native peoples who once lived in the Deep South told stories, too. And they, too, have a trickster rabbit, who appears in the Creek tale "Nuts! Nuts! Nuts!" To my mind, his behavior is very much like the antic misdoings of that other rascally hare!

In addition to all these stories, I've included lots of rhymes, riddles, and superstitions. It's hard to pinpoint exactly where each is from, for they're told all over the South. For instance, though "Did You Feed My Cow?"—a hand-clapping, toe-tapping, back-and-forth, give-and-take choral chant—was first recorded off the Carolina coast, it can be heard clear over to Mississippi.

Believe me, I had an especially hard time choosing which superstitions to include here. All are just too funny for words—and deeply embedded in the souls of every Southerner. To this day, my mother won't let a black cat cross her path if she can help it—and neither will I!

So pretend you're sittin' on a porch somewhere in the Deep South—and let the words drip off the page as you tell these tales.

# I Had a Little Dog

I had a little dog.
His name was Pug
Every time he ran,
He went jug, jug, jug.

I had a little dog.
His name was Trot.
He held up his tail
All tied in a knot.

I had a little dog.
His name was Blue.
I put him on the road,
And he almost flew.

I had a little dog.
His name was Rover.
When he died,
He died all over.

# Bat

Bat! Bat! Come under my hat,
And I'll give you a slice o' bacon.
But don't bring none of your ol' bedbugs,
If you don't want to get forsaken.

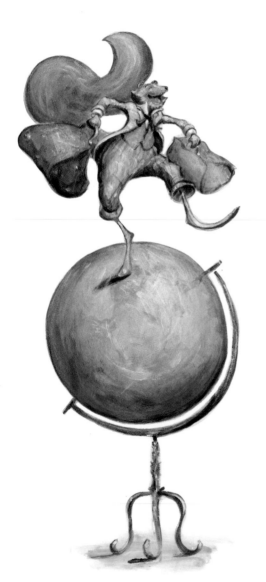

# The Squirrel

Of all the beasts that roam the woods,
I'd rather be a squirrel.
Curl my tail upon my back,
And travel all over the world.

# The Big Dinin'

As usual, Brer Rabbit is up to his ol' tricks. But this time, Brer Frog is determined to outsmart him.

Brer Frog knows how much Brer Rabbit loves fried fish. So the first thing Brer Frog does is he holds a big dinin' with everybody invited—except Brer Rabbit.

When Brer Rabbit hears about this, he is ready to have a fit, he's so mad. But Brer Rabbit, he won't let on, oh no, not at all.

Meanwhile Brer Frog, he feels dead sure that Brer Rabbit will come anyway. So he fixes up a special table right on the water, just a-waitin' there for Brer Rabbit.

On the way to the big dinin', everyone passes by Brer Rabbit.

"Evenin', Brer Rabbit," says Brer Coon. "Aren't you comin' to the big dinin'?"

"No," says Brer Rabbit. "I'd rather dine on corn bread and water than eat what Brer Frog cooks."

So Brer Coon goes along by himself.

"Evenin', Brer Rabbit," says Brer Fox. "Aren't you comin' to the big dinin'?"

27

"No," says Brer Rabbit. "I'd rather drink a gallon of castor oil than eat one itty-bitty ol' nasty-tastin' fish that Brer Frog cooks."

So Brer Fox passes him by, too.

Directly, Brer Rabbit sniffs the night air. He can smell that fish fryin', he sure can. *Sniff! Sniff!* His nose is about to fall off, it's sniffin' that hard. Why, Brer Rabbit feels likely to pass out if he doesn't get some of that fried fish to eat soon.

Off he goes, trippety-trippin' over to the branch to take a peek. *Aaaw!* Would you take a look at that! There's ol' Brer Frog as busy as can be, hoppin' from one fryin' pan to the other, keepin' twenty fires goin' all at once. Sure enough, everybody is there except Brer Rabbit, and they are havin' themselves a good ol' time.

By now Brer Rabbit can't hardly see straight, he's so mad. He's going to trick them or his name ain't Brer Rabbit, that's all there is to it.

The next thing you know, there's the most ornery sound you ever did hear risin' up out of the swamp. 'Course, you know who it is, don't you?

*OOOOOOOOOHHH-AAAAAAHHHH-OOOOOOOOOO!*

"What's that!" says Brer Coon.

"Did you hear that?" says Brer Fox.

*OOOOOOOOOOHHHH-AAAAAAAHHHH-OOOOOOOOOO!*

"There it goes again!" says Brer Possum.

"Sounds like a ghost, if you ask me," says Brer Bear.

That's all anybody has to say. Nothin' on earth is scarier than a hant, no sirree.

*Plop! Splash!* Brer Frog and Brer Turtle hide under the water.

Lickety-split! All the other critters light out for home as fast as their four legs will carry them.

*Dum dee dum dum dum*. . . . Here comes ol' Brer Rabbit, takin' his own sweet time, hoppin' from one table to the next, fillin' his belly full of good-tastin' fried fish.

"Shame to let all this go to waste," he says, licking his whiskers.

Now Brer Rabbit doesn't see two great big ol' round eyes pop out of the water. They happen to belong to none other than Brer Frog. He's a-sittin' and a-waitin' and a-watchin' Brer Rabbit. Oh yes, he's a-catchin' a good show!

Meanwhile Brer Rabbit cleans up all the tables but one. He's been savin' this one for last. It has the biggest pile of fish on it he ever did see. Don't you know, it's the one Brer Frog had specially laid out for him. Brer Rabbit has no idea it's just a plank a-floatin' on top of the water.

With a run and a leap, Brer Rabbit lands smack dab in the middle of the plank. Whoopsy-doodle! Into the water he goes with a great big *ker-splash!* And that big ol' platter of fried fish lands right in front of Brer Frog.

"Oho, Brer Rabbit," says Brer Frog, "you are mighty kind to fetch me my dinner."

"*Glub! Glub! Glub!* Help me, Brer Frog," sputters Brer Rabbit. (Rabbits are not known for their swimming ability, don't you know.)

"Um-ummm!" says Brer Frog. "This is the mightiest, finest-tastin' fried fish I ever did eat, if I do say so myself."

*"Glub! Glub! Glub!"* says Brer Rabbit, a-dunkin' and a-splashin' in the deep water.

"What's that you say, Brer Rabbit?" asks Brer Frog.

"I say—*sputter sputter*—Brer Frog—*sputter sputter*—get me out of the water—*sputter sputter*—if you don't mind," says Brer Rabbit, barely able to breathe.

"It's Master Brer Frog to you," says Brer Frog. "And if I get you out, you have to do whatever I tell you to do."

"Will do, Master Brer Frog—*gulp!*—I promise—*gulp,"* says Brer Rabbit.

So Brer Frog, he helps Brer Rabbit to shore.

And Brer Rabbit gets busy washin' all the dinner dishes, he sure does.

And Brer Frog, he just sits there feeling as proud as he can be for havin' outsmarted one smart-alecky ol' rabbit!

*Tin's bent—
story's endt!*

# The Watermelon

That ham bone and chicken are sweet.
That possum meat is sure fine.
But give to me—now, don't you cheat—
That watermelon smilin' on the vine.

# The Watermillion Patch

Brer Rabbit and Brer Coon are always in cahoots. Why, they stick together like two hoecakes on a plate of molasses, they do. When one falls down, the other picks him up and dusts him off, if you know what I mean. I reckon that's how it's always been.

On this one particular gloriously fine morning, Brer Rabbit and Brer Coon are feelin' mighty pleased with themselves, they sure are. And the reason they feel this way is because, for more days than they can count, the two have been a-workin'. They've worn themselves to a frazzle, a-diggin' and a-plantin' and a-hoein'. But law, look how it has paid off.

Now Brer Rabbit and Brer Coon have the grandest patch of watermelons you ever did see! Did I say "watermelon"? No, no, no, these are no ordinary everyday run-of-the-mill variety of watermelon, no sirree. These are water*millions,* the *finest* of the *finest, the one in a million* kind that nobody, lookin' high or low, could ever expect to find growin' here, there, or anywhere else. That's right, these melons are fine enough to suit up and sit beside you at Sunday dinner.

But hold on a minute now. Who's that a-creepin' along the fence on his tippy toes, like he's afraid he might step on a snake and wake it up? Unh-unh! It's Colonel Tiger, and he's a-lookin' mighty hungry, he sure is. Matter of fact, he looks hungry enough to eat up Brer Rabbit, Brer Coon, and that whole patch of watermillions, skin and all; yes, he sure does.

And, don't you know, before Brer Rabbit can blink an eye, that ol' Brer Coon is a-scrambly-scramblin' up the only tree he can find. Humph! Brer Rabbit is not pleased one bit to be left standing there all by his lonesome.

Believe you me, that ol' Brer Rabbit would just as soon hightail it up the tree along with ol' Brer Coon . . . that is, if he knew how. But Brer Rabbit doesn't know the first thing about climbin' trees, he sure doesn't. Unh-unh. Now he has to do some serious thinkin'.

When he sees that ol' Tiger movin' closer, Brer Rabbit does what Brer Rabbit does best. He grabs a spade and a-diggety-diga-diggin' he goes, as fast as all get out. And he makes two great big ol' holes in the ground.

Into these great big ol' holes Brer Rabbit rolls two great big ol' watermillions. *Pa-lumph! Pa-lumph!* He covers them up quick, then pats the dirt ever so gently, like a baby's bottom, smoothing it with the underside of his spade, just so.

By the time Colonel Tiger arrives at the gate, oh my! Brer Rabbit has gone ahead and dug another hole, deep enough to hold something real big.

*Hmmmm . . .* Ol' Tiger, he's just a-standin' there in his fine striped suit, a-tuggin' on his long, woolly whiskers, just a-watchin' Brer Rabbit—and a-wonderin' mighty hard.

*Hmmmm . . .* Ol' Tiger, he's a mite curious, he is, just a-wonderin' who exactly is planted in those two big ol' graves Brer Rabbit has dug.

*Hmmmm . . .* Ol' Tiger, he is even curiouser, he is, just a-wantin' to know who exactly Brer Rabbit plans to put in that brand-new freshly dug grave that just so happens to be about his size.

Havin' looked over the situation, Colonel Tiger decides he has stood all he can stand, so he says to Brer Rabbit, "Brer Rabbit," he says, "what, exactly, what is it that you are a-doin'?"

Brer Rabbit won't let on how scared he is, oh no. His fur is jumpin' up at attention, he's that scared, but he acts like he's mad, don't you know. "Why, I'm a-buryin' all the folks I've killed today," he says. He hits the graves hard with his spade. *Slap! Slap!*

"Right here"—*slap!*— "is Brer Lion and right here"—*slap!*— "is Brer Bear."

"Is that a fact?" says Colonel Tiger, feeling just a wee bit shaky in the middle. "You don't say."

"I do say," says Brer Rabbit. "And if you looky up in that tree over yonder, you'll see Brer Coon. He's next."

"Sure enough?" says Colonel Tiger, feelin' mighty uncomfortable now.

"And," says Brer Rabbit, "if you don't stop askin' me so many fool questions, Brer Tiger, I'm afraid I'll just have to add you to my list."

"Much obliged," says Colonel Tiger, backin' off. "But I don't believe I'll be needin' to stay here much longer." The next thing you know, he's taken off like he was stung in the tail. Quick as a wink, he's put a mile or two between him and that dangus-talkin' Brer Rabbit.

Seein' the coast is clear, Brer Coon slides back down the tree and saunters over to Brer Rabbit, full of admiration for his friend. "Oh, Brer Rabbit, you are somethin' else! Did you see how ol' Brer Tiger ran off? You are one mighty smart rabbit, sure enough."

"Don't even talk to me," says Brer Rabbit. "I'm dividin' up this patch of watermillions right now. Take all you can tote away and get out of here."

"All I can tote away?" says Brer Coon.

"You heard me," says Brer Rabbit. "Since I'm the littlest, I'll just keep what's left behind."

Well now, Brer Coon can only lift up one little ol' itty-bitty watermillion and with that, he has to go off. This means the whole entire patch of watermillions, minus one little ol' itty-bitty one, now belongs to Brer Rabbit.

But Brer Coon pays this no mind. He eyes that big ol' hole Brer Rabbit dug, just a-sittin' there empty as can be, just a-waitin' to be full of somethin'—or someone!—and off he goes. That's right, Brer Coon is mighty thankful to be gettin' as far away as he can from this mighty powerful Brer Rabbit. And that's the truth!

*I stepped on a piece of tin;*
*The tin bended,*
*My story ended.*

# The Egg

I had a chicken.
It grew so tall,
It took a month
For the egg to fall.

# The Rooster

I had a little rooster.
He crowed before day.
Long came a big owl
And toted him away.

The rooster fought hard,
So the owl let him go.
Now all the pretty hens
Want that rooster for their beau!

# Country Riddles

A duck behind a duck.
A duck before a duck.
A duck between a duck.
How many ducks?
   *(three)*

Opens like a barn door,
Shuts up like a bat.
Guess all your lifetime,
You'll never guess that.
   *(an umbrella)*

Four legs up and four legs
down, soft in the middle,
and hard all 'round.
   *(a bed)*

What flies high, flies low,
but doesn't have wings?
   *(dust)*

Round as a biscuit,
Deep as a cup,
All the king's horses
Can't pull it up.

*(a well)*

The man that made it never used it.
The man that used it never saw it.

*(a coffin)*

Runs all around the house and makes
one track.

*(a wheelbarrow)*

A houseful, a yardful,
And can't catch a
spoonful.

*(smoke)*

# The Old Hen Cackled

The old hen she cackled
And stayed in the barn.
She got fat and sassy
A-eatin' up the corn.

The old hen she cackled,
Got great yellow legs.
She swallowed down the oats,
But I didn't get no eggs.

The old hen she cackled,
She cackled in the lot.
The next time she cackled,
She cackled in the pot.

# Ol' Mister Biggety

*"Cockley-doodly-doo!"* crows Mister Rooster. He struts around the barnyard lookin' as proud as he can be. And he makes sure everybody *treats* him like a king, too. He tosses those tail feathers about like whips to remind everybody who's boss. Don't forget Mister Rooster has a loud say, if you know what I mean. That *cockley-doodly-doo* of his gets the whole barnyard out of bed at sunup. "Rise and shine!" says Mister Rooster. "Time to get to work."

On this one fine day, the whole barnyard is a-cacklin', a-gabbin', and a-quackin' in anticipation. The neighbors are holdin' a big supper dance, and anybody who has a beak and no teeth is welcome to come.

Of course, it's Mister Rooster who leads the way. With a great big *cockley-doodly-doo*, he gathers the whole flock together. Behind Mister Rooster comes ol' lady Hen and Miss Pullet.

Then comes Mister Turkey Gobbler, Miss Guinea Hen, Mister Peafowl and Miss Puddle Duck, and off they march. That Mister Rooster, he struts out front like a drum major leadin' a marchin' band, showin' off his pretty colors.

Right off, as soon as they all get there, ol' fiddler Goose sets a-playin'. They all have to dance a spell to work up a good appetite. Then, after doe-si-doein' a dozen rounds or so, the hens, geese, ducks, and gobblers file into the supper room—led by Mister Rooster, of course.

But what do you suppose they find? Why, it appears that what

is being served for supper is nothin' more than plain ol' corn bread, piled twice as high as the old gobbler's head.

"I declare," squawks Mister Rooster. "This here is the sorriest feast I ever did see." Feelin' mighty indignant, he struts out, sayin', "I'll have nothin' to do with so mean a supper. Why, I can get all the corn bread I want at home."

When ol' Miss Guinea Hen sees this, she hollers out, *"Pot-rack! Pot-rack!* Mister Rooster's gone back!"

*"Cackly-cack!"* says ol' lady Hen.

*"Gobbly-gobble!"* says Mister Turkey Gobbler.

And Miss Puddle Duck, she shakes her tail and says, *"Quickity-quickity-quack!"*

This time nobody follows Mister Rooster. Everybody's too hungry, so they stay and eat. *Peck! Peck! Peck!* They work through the first layer in no time at all. And guess what they find underneath? More corn bread? Unh-unh! They find bacon! Unh-huh! Greens! Unh-huh! Sweet potatoes! Unh-huh! And, on the bottom, more dishes of pies and cakes and good things to eat than you ever did see.

Mister Rooster hasn't gone far when he hears all the carryin' on, so he peeks through a crack. And my, oh, my, when he sees all the good dinin' he's a-missin' he almost has a fit. But he can't go back on his word, oh law, no. Mister Rooster, he's so mighty biggety and stuck-up, he just struts off.

Still, Mister Rooster sure has learned his lesson. Now wherever he finds food, Mister Rooster scratches and scratches, first with his left foot, then with his right, and sometimes with both. Yes sir, Mister Rooster scratches and never leaves off scratchin' until he is sure he has struck rock bottom.

> *I stepped on a piece of tin,*
> *The tin bent,*
> *That's how my story went.*

## The Mule

I had a little mule, and his name was Jack.
I rode on his tail to save his back.
This little mule, he kicked so high,
I thought that I had touched the sky!

## The Goat

A goat one day was feeling fine.
He ate ten shirts from off the line.

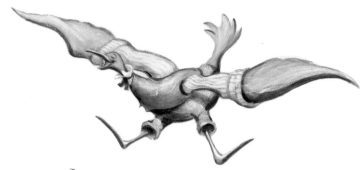

## MiSTer BuZZard

Oh, Mister Buzzard, don't you fly so high.
You can't get your livin' flyin' high in the sky.

# How Come Ol' Buzzard Boards

Every bird has a nest but one. Ol' Buzzard, he has to board when it comes time to roost. That's right, he has to shop around and find a nest that's not occupied if and when he wants to raise a family. If he weren't so biggety and persnickety, he might have had a home to call his own. Here's the story of how Ol' Buzzard lost his chance when the pickin's were good.

Way in the back-before time, when birds had no comfy places to call their own, an honest-to-goodness nestin' tree sprung up out of nowhere. It was round and plump and full of every kind of nest you could imagine. Why, nests were just a-hangin' there, ripe and ready to pick. Down below was a big sign sayin', FIRST TO COME, FIRST TO CHOOSE.

Well, when Ol' Buzzard saw this sign, he went a-step-a-steppin', *hop-a-hop, kerflop,* lookin' over the whole lot, don't you know.

Then Ol' Buzzard said,

    "No, thank you—none!

    Not one! Not one!"

He stuck his big ol' ugly head into the softest, prettiest nest and looked first with one eye, then the other.

    "You call this good, do you?

    I don't, for true! For true!"

The other birds couldn't believe he was actin' so uppity. They called out to Ol' Buzzard,

> "Yes! Yes! Yes!
>
> A very nice nest!"

But Ol' Buzzard just stood there.

Hummingbird, she zipped down and grabbed up that nest and flew off with it.

Ol' Buzzard just a-hopped, *kerflop,* to the next nest and laughed.

> "Haw! Haw! Haw!
>
> Caw! Caw! Caw!"

Oriole came by. "What's so funny?"

Ol' Buzzard croaked,

> "Haw! Haw! Haw! Haw!
>
> The funniest nest I ever saw!"

Oriole didn't care. She grabbed that nest like it was the grand prize and flew off with it.

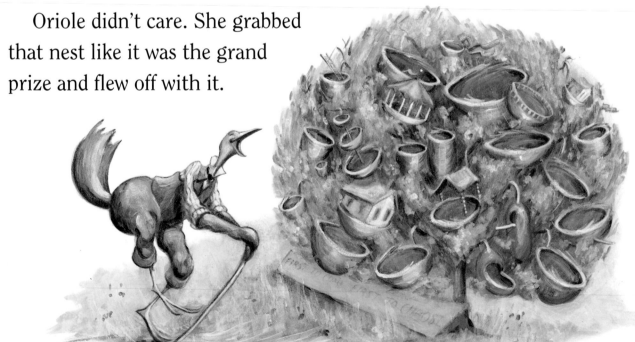

Next, Thrush flew down. She had her eye on another one and sang out,

> "A pretty nest!
> The very best!"

Ol' Buzzard just laughed.

> "Pretty house? Pretty house?
> It isn't fit for even a mouse."

But Thrush grabbed it up and flew off, singin',

> "Maybe! Maybe!
> But it suits me. Suits me!"

Finally Mockingbird came along. There was only one nest left. It was a raggedy one made out of a bundle of sticks.

Ol' Buzzard laughed.

> "That's a bundle of sticks—
> In a mighty poor fix.
> I could knock it to pieces
> In just two licks!"

Mockingbird looked at Ol' Buzzard. She sang out,

> "How come you laugh so?
> Laugh so! Oho!
> Laugh so! Oho!"

Buzzard croaked,

> "I laugh at that home;
> I'd rather roam,
> Than live in that home!"

Mockingbird shook her head and flew off. Even though her new nest was mighty rough, she made it into the sweetest home of all with her singin'.

Because Buzzard was actin' so persnickety, all the birds called out,

> "Oh! Oh! Oh! Oh!
> You let the time past!
> That was the last!"

Now Ol' Buzzard, he started feelin' mighty bad, but he pretended not to be sorry at all. He went a-step-a-steppin', *hop-hop, kerplop,* onto the fence and there he stayed. That's where you'll find him. With no home, Ol' Buzzard is obliged to roam. So when you catch a glimpse of him a-seesawin' up in the sky, you know he's just a-floatin' around, lookin' for a place to board.

> *I go around a bend,*
> *To see a fence to mend.*
> *On it's hung my story's end.*

# Did You Feed My Cow?

"Did you feed my cow?"
"Yes, Ma'am!"
"Will you tell me how?"
"Yes, Ma'am!"
"Oh, what did you give her?"
"Corn and hay."
"Oh, what did you give her?"
"Corn and hay."

"Did you milk her good?"
"Yes, Ma'am!"
"Did you do like you should?"
"Yes, Ma'am!"
"Oh, how did you milk her?"
"Swish! Swish! Swish!"
"Oh, how did you milk her?"
"Swish! Swish! Swish!"

"Did that cow die?"
"Yes, Ma'am!"
"With a pain in her eye?"
"Yes, Ma'am!"
"Oh, how did she die?"
"Uh! Uh! Uh!"

"Oh, how did she die?"
"Uh! Uh! Uh!"

"Did the buzzards come?"
"Yes, Ma'am!"
"For to pick her bones?"
"Yes, Ma'am!"
"Oh, how did they come?"
"Flop! Flop! Flop!"
"Oh, how did they come?"
"Flop! Flop! Flop!"
"Flop! Flop! Flop!"
"Flop! Flop! Flop!"
"Flop! Flop! Flop!"

# Nobody Likes Me

I like nobody.
Nobody likes me.
But I'm as happy as I can be.
I'll always be single,
always be free,
Because I like nobody,
And nobody likes me.

# Poor Little Kitty

Poor little kitty cat,
Poor little feller,
Poor little kitty cat
Died in the cellar.

# Mister Grumpy Rides the clouds

Now, why do you suppose everybody once called Brer Terrapin "Mister Grumpy"? Let me tell you. Because he earned that name, that's why.

Brer Terrapin used to be a grumblin' and a fussin' kind of character. And it was just because he had to creep along close to the ground.

When he met up with Brer Rabbit, do you know what Mister Grumpy did?

He grumbled, that's what. 'Cause Mister Grumpy couldn't run as fast as the wind like Brer Rabbit. No sirree, he sure couldn't.

And when he met up with Brer Buzzard, do you know what Mister Grumpy did? He fussed, that's what. 'Cause Mister Grumpy couldn't fly in the clouds like Brer Buzzard. No sirree, he sure couldn't.

It got so nobody could stand listenin' to Mister Grumpy and his bad mouth, a-fumin' and a-fussin' and a-carryin' on like that. So right then and there, the folks decided to put a stop to it.

"It's about time somebody taught him a thing or two," said Brer Buzzard.

Sure enough, when Mister Grumpy met up with Miss Crow, he started carryin' on to beat the band. But this time, guess what?

Miss Crow said as sweetly as beet sugar, "Oh, Brer Terrapin, don't worry. I'm gon' cheer you up! How'd you like to ride the clouds?"

"Whoo-ee!" said Mister Grumpy. "Ride the clouds, Miss Crow? Hot diggety-dee, indeed I would!"

Off they went a-sailin' high up in the sky, a-swoopin' here, a-swoopin' there, every which a-way.

When Mister Grumpy looked down below, he saw all the folks jumpin' and clappin', tossin' their hats into the air, and a course he thought they were applaudin' *him*. Yes sirree, Mister Grumpy was mighty proud of himself. He had no idea those folks could hardly wait to see Miss Crow drop Mister Grumpy, *smack! splat!*

Did she? Unh-huh, she sure did. Down went Mister Grumpy like a big ol' rock and he landed . . . *plop!* on top of Brer Buzzard. And Brer Buzzard was not very happy, no sirree. He decided to take Mister Grumpy on a ride he would never forget.

Brer Buzzard shot straight up like a cannonball heading directly for the sun. "Hold on to your head, Brer Terrapin," he warned. "Or it might fall off!" Then, fast as lightnin', Brer Buzzard zippity-dooed back down again.

Meanwhile Mister Grumpy, he was a-thinkin' that creepin' along the ground sounded like a mighty fine thing to be doing. "Oh, kindly take me back, Brer Buzzard," he begged. "I've had enough a flyin', thank you very much."

"You have?" said Brer Buzzard. "Well, I'm tickled to hear that, Brer Terrapin." With a flick of his tail, he sent Mister Grumpy

a-tumblin'. Down Mister Grumpy went like a big ol' chunk of clay and he landed . . . *plop!* on top of King Eagle.

"I do declare," said King Eagle. "What a surprise!"

"Oh, King Eagle," said Mister Grumpy. "I beg you, *puh-leeze,* don't dump me. Just take me back down to the ground."

"Did you ride a cloud yet?" said King Eagle.

"Oh no, no clouds," said Mister Grumpy. "But that's all right. I don't need to ride any ol' cloud."

"But ridin' clouds is the best part of flyin'," said King Eagle.

This time when Mister Grumpy looked down, he about passed out. Why, the folks below looked like itty-bitty ants runnin' around trees that poked out of the ground like a bunch of tooth-picks.

"Oh, puh-leeze have mercy, King Eagle," cried Mister Grumpy. "Put me down!"

But King Eagle paid him no mind at all. Up he climbed, a-flappin' his great wings until they rode the clouds, which hung in the sky thick as fresh-picked cotton.

Mister Grumpy, he was mighty tired. And was he scared? Oh yes, unh-huh, he was mighty scared. He figured King Eagle was headin' straight for heaven and had no plans for stoppin' before then.

All of a sudden Mister Grumpy had a remembrance. Sure enough, when he reached into his pocket, he found a spool of thread he had bought for his wife. So he tied one end around

King Eagle's leg and grabbed hold. Then, slow-like, he let himself slip down, *z-zimp, z-zimp.*

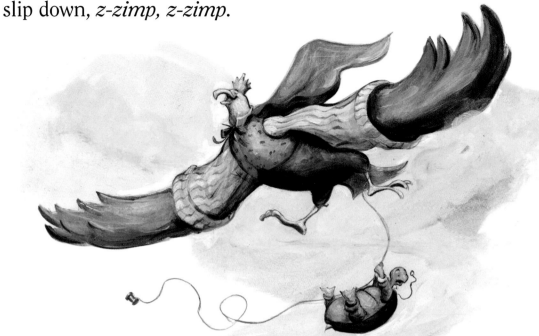

SNAP! The thread broke.

WHAM! Mister Grumpy hit the ground *hard.*

When he woke up, you know what? He wasn't Mister Grumpy anymore. Unh-uh. He was Brer Terrapin. *Just* Brer Terrapin. Now, could Brer Terrapin run? No sirree. Could Brer Terrapin fly? No, unh-uh, not at all. But could he crawl? You better believe it!

That's right, he crawls and he crawls, with such satisfaction, folks are sure to think this is all he has ever had in his mind to do. HAH!

> *Biddy, biddy, bend,*
> *My story is end.*
> *Turn loose the rooster*
> *And hold down the hen.*

# The Bee

The bee he is an insect small,
And cunning like a weasel;
And when he lands upon you-all,
He leaves a little measle.

# The Grasshopper

There was a little grasshopper
That was always on the jump,
And 'cause he never looked ahead
He always got a bump.

# Nuts! Nuts! Nuts!

Rabbit and Panther *used* to be good friends. But they argued all the time. If one said no, the other said yes. Always. No matter what.

One day they went off to visit friend Bear. Bear lived way, way up the river, far off in the distant hills. Even though big Panther took his time walking along, poor little Rabbit had to hop-hop twice as fast just to keep up. It wore him out.

But when Panther came to a creek and said, "Let's stop here for the night, friend Rabbit," did Rabbit say yes?

Rabbit, huffing and puffing, ready to drop if he had to hop another hop, said, "No!" Did that make sense? No, it didn't, but if one said yes, the other said *no*. Always. No matter what.

"Why not?" asked Panther.

"This creek is haunted," said Rabbit. This is what Rabbit told Panther. He made it up.

"No, it isn't," said Panther.

"Yes, it is," said Rabbit.

"No, it isn't!"

"Yes, it is!"

"No, it isn't!"

"Yes, it is," said Rabbit. "Anybody who sleeps by the creek will get burned alive."

"Humph!" said Panther. "We're going to camp here, no matter what!"

Rabbit was angry. And on the spot he hatched a plan to get back at Panther. You see, Rabbit knew that Panther might be bigger, but he certainly wasn't smarter.

"You'll be sorry," said Rabbit.

"No, I won't!"

"Yes, you will!"

"No, I won't!"

"Yes, you will!"

"Good night, friend Rabbit," said Panther.

"Good night," said Rabbit.

After a moment he said, "Oh, friend Panther, what kind of noise do you make when you sleep?"

"When I sleep?" said Panther. "Why, I say, *'Nutslagum! Nutslagum! Nutslagum!'* when I sleep. What do you say when you sleep, friend Rabbit?"

"What do I say when I sleep?" said Rabbit. "Why, I say *'Nuts! Nuts! Nuts!'* when I sleep, friend Panther."

"Why do you ask?" said Panther, yawning a loud *hah-hum.*

"Just wondered, that's all," said Rabbit. It looked like he was trying very hard to stay awake.

"Well, good night, friend Rabbit," said Panther, all curled up with his eyes shut.

"Good night, friend Panther," said Rabbit. "Sleep well," he added, chuckling to himself.

In a short time, Rabbit pretended to snore, muttering, *"Nuts! Nuts! Nuts!"*

Thinking that Rabbit was sound asleep, Panther nodded off, snoring, *"Nutslagum! Nutslagum! Nutslagum!"*

When Rabbit heard this, he hopped up. Quickly he found a piece of bark and shoveled hot coals from the fire onto it. He threw the whole thing on Panther, then jumped back into bed, snoring loudly, *"Nuts! Nuts! Nuts!"*

Panther jumped up and howled with pain. "OW! OWOOOOOO!"

He shook Rabbit. "Wake up, friend Rabbit, wake up!"

Rabbit pretended to be angry. "What is wrong with you! Why did you shake me awake like that?"

"Friend Rabbit," said Panther. "You were right. This is a terrible place!"

"I told you so, I told you so!" said Rabbit. Then he pretended to fall right back to sleep. *"Nuts! Nuts! Nuts!"* snored Rabbit, as loudly as he could.

Hearing this, Panther settled down once more with a loud snore. *"Nutslagum! Nutslagum! Nutslagum!"*

When Rabbit heard this, he hopped up and played the same trick again.

But Panther was only pretending to sleep. He watched as Rabbit gathered hot coals on a piece of bark. When Rabbit was about to toss it, Panther jumped up. "AHA!"

With a giant hop, Rabbit just barely escaped the claws of his furious friend. And to this day they no longer speak. They no longer say no to each other or yes to each other. Never. No matter what. In fact, panthers eat rabbits whenever they can catch them.

*This is for true.*

# We Hunted and We Hollered

So we hunted and we hollered and the first thing we find
Was a barn in the meadows, and that we left behind.
One say it was a barn, and the other say, "Nay!"
They all say a church with the steeple washed away.

So we hunted and we hollered and the second thing we find
Was a cow in the meadow, and that we left behind.
One say it was a cow, and the other say, "Nay!"
They all say it was an elephant with its snout washed away.

So we hunted and we hollered and the third thing we find
Was an owl in the ivy bush, and that we left behind.
One say it was an owl, and the other say, "Nay!"
They all say it was the devil and we all ran away.

# What You Got There?

What you got there?
Bread and cheese.
Where's my share?
In the wood.
Where's the wood?
Fire burned it down.
Where's the fire?
Water put it out.
Where's the water?
Ox drunk it.
Where's the ox?
Butcher killed it.
Where's the butcher?
Rope hung him.
Where's the rope?
Rat gnawed it.
Where's the rat?
Cat caught it.
Where's the cat?
Dead and buried behind the old church door.
Fee fo, first um speaks or shows his teeth
Gets a pinch and a smack or a slap.

# Superstitions

Stepping over a broom is bad luck. Undo
it by stepping backwards over the broom.

Don't let a black
cat cross your
path or you'll
have bad luck.

Wear red flannel to cure aching bones.

Bad luck it is to begin work on Friday.

Don't sing out before breakfast,
Don't sing out before you eat,
Or you'll cry out before midnight,
You'll cry before you sleep.

If a buzzard flies over your house, you are going to get good news.

Hang a dead snake on a bush or fence to bring rain.

To cure an earache, stew some earthworms and use the fat.

To find a spider on your overclothes is good luck.

# NIGHTY-NIGHT RHYMES

## Good Night

Good night, sleep tight,
Don't let the bedbugs bite.
If they do, take your shoe,
Hit them till they're black and blue!

# The Fly

Baby bye, here's a fly;
Let us watch him, you and I.
How he crawls on the walls,
Yet he never falls.
If you and I had six such legs
We could surely walk on eggs.
There he goes, on his toes,
Tickling baby's nose!

# Little Horsies

Go to sleepy, little baby!
When you awake,
I'll give you angel cake
And a whole lot of little horsies:
One will be red,
One will be blue,
One will be the color of your nanny's shoe.

71

# PART III
# Up and Round the Mountains

Nestled deep in the hollows of the Great Smokies and Blue Ridge Mountains, there are tiny pockets of kinfolk who still make their own clothes and furnishings, grow their own food, and build their own homes. In this area known as Appalachia, there are still a few strong, independent folks who have lived long enough to remember the old ways of doing things. But the younger folks are caught up with progress and all its modern conveniences. Living the simple life is no longer a necessity for many of them, so the old ways are fast disappearing.

One thing, though, hasn't changed at all. Everybody there still loves to tell or listen to a good story. This is where a tale is stretched to its limits, sometimes taking an hour or more to tell. There used to be a good reason for it: telling stories was a way to get everybody's minds off their chores. While listening, folks'd be busy string-beaning, corn shucking, barn raising, quilt making, and so forth. Of course, storytelling also kept the young'uns quiet while they helped out, too. Nowadays, the sole purpose of storytelling is pure enjoyment, with no strings attached.

Many of these tales came from England, Ireland, Scotland, or Germany, where the ancestors of the mountain folk once lived. When the descendents settled into their rugged, isolated new American homeland, the tales were recast with a different assortment of characters more like themselves. Though the whole world may know the English folktale "Jack the Giant Killer," it's completely different from the version mountain folk tell. Like many other old familiar-sounding stories, it somehow got a face-lift when it passed through these mountains. Take "Jack Runs Off," for instance, which is included in this section. It may remind you of an old German folktale called "The Bremen Town Musicians," only it sure doesn't *sound* the same. That's because it's been refined by the mountain folks who now claim this version as their own.

Tales are still handed down in traditional fashion, from one generation to the next. For instance, Mrs. Maud Long of Hot Springs, North Carolina, first heard the Jack tales

73

from her mother, Mrs. Jane Hicks Gentry, who had learned them from her mother, who had in turn heard them from her father, Council Harmon. As these tales trickled down, they were changed again and again, depending on who told them. The silly, tongue-twisting tale "Three Foots" is a good example of this; I've heard at least four versions, and now here's yet another!

Most poetry from Appalachia is put to music. Just listen to any of the beautiful ballads or lively folk tunes, now played and sung the world over. And music coupled with a lively dance is pretty standard fare at most get-togethers where stories are shared. More often than not, a listener pulls out a fiddle or has a dulcimer handy, then anybody can join in on the refrains of a story like "Ol' Gally Mander" and sing along, too. Half sung, half told, "Gally" is a far-fetched version of an English tale called "The Old Witch."

There are also plenty of superstitions still hanging around, some told with a laugh, but more often in earnest. The old-timers tend to perpetuate these sayings by repeating them often—to anyone who will listen!

So, have a good chuckle as you read these hand-me-downs that rooted themselves on the side of one of those big ol' mountains tucked away in the clouds, far off from just about anywhere.

# Ol' Man Dan

Ol' Man Dan was a tough ol' man;
Washed his face with a fryin' pan,
Combed his hair with a wagon wheel,
Died with a toothache in his heel.

# Ol' Gally Mander

Ol' Gally Mander was a stingy ol' hag and nasty to boot. She was so lazy, she kept hirin' girls all the time to come in and clean. Most didn't stay but a second, 'cause they couldn't stand her.

But one day a girl came along who was as stingy and nasty as ol' Gally Mander. Fact is, they took to each other right well. After a time, ol' Gally Mander decided she could trust to leave this gal alone to clean house while she went off a-visitin'. Just before she went out the door, ol' Gally Mander said,

> "You can scrub-a-dub and rub-a-rub,
> But don't peek up my chimney!"

"I wouldn't think of doin' somethin' like that," said the girl.

Course, as soon as ol' Gally Mander went out, that's the first thing this hag of a girl did. She got down on her hands and knees and peeked up the chimney.

"What's that?" she said, poking around with a stick. Then with a *plop,* a long leather purse fell, *drop,* right into her hands.

Why, it was full of gold and silver!

"Whoo-ee!" Off she ran as fast as her two skinny legs would take her.

Directly, she passed an old cow. It called out,

"Hey, pretty gal, don't act like a hag,
Come milk my sore ol' milkin' bag."

But the girl said,

"I've got no time to fool with you, honey.
I'm goin' round the world with all this money!"

Then off she ran. Went on a little way and met a horse. It called out,

>"Hey, pretty gal, don't run anymore.
>
>Please rub my back 'cause it's mighty sore."

But the girl said,

>"I've got no time to fool with you, honey.
>
>I'm goin' round the world with all this money!"

Off she ran some more. Further down the road she met a peach tree. It called out,

>"Hey, pretty gal, before you go,
>
>Come pick my peaches 'cause my limbs hurt so."

But the girl said,

>"I've got no time to fool with you, honey.
>
>I'm goin' round the world with all this money!"

Then off she ran.

Meanwhile, ol' Gally Mander had come back and found the girl gone and her purse gone. She took off down the road, hollerin',

>"Gally Mander, Gally Mander, what could be worse!
>
>That gal's run off with my long leather purse!"

She loopdy-looped down the road and met the old cow.

>"Ol' cow," said she, "did a gal run by?
>
>She stole my purse, and that's no lie!"

The cow shook her bony head and said, "She went thataway."
Ol' Gally Mander ran off, hollerin',

>"Gally Mander, Gally Mander, what could be worse!
>
>That gal's run off with my long leather purse!"

She stumbly-bumbled down the road and met the old horse.

"Ol' horse," said she, "did a gal run by?

She stole my purse, and that's no lie!"

The horse swatted his tangly tail and said, "She went thataway."

Ol' Gally Mander ran off, hollerin',

"Gally Mander, Gally Mander, what could be worse!

That gal's run off with my long leather purse!"

She ran lickety-split down the road and met the peach tree.

"Ol' tree," said she, "did a gal run by?

She stole my purse and that's no lie!"

The peach tree wriggled its topmost limb and said, "She went thataway."

Ol' Gally Mander ran off, hollerin',

"Gally Mander, Gally Mander, what could be worse!

That gal's run off with my long leather purse!"

Soon she came to the ocean where, at last, she found the girl. She grabbed her purse, then tossed the screaming hag of a girl into the salty sea.

Before you know it, ol' Gally Mander had gone and hired a new girl. This one was much too nice to work for the likes of her. But she did. By and by, ol' Gally Mander left the girl alone while she went off a-visitin'. 'Course, she told her the same thing she'd told t'other.

"You can scrub-a-dub and rub-a-rub,

But don't peek up my chimney!"

"I wouldn't think of doin' somethin' like that," said the girl— and she meant it. Only thing was, ol' Gally Mander didn't come back for the longest time, and this poor girl thought somethin' terrible had happened. So she started a-cleanin' like crazy and without thinkin' stuck her broom up the chimney.

*Plop! Drop!* Down fell the long leather purse.

"Oh, dear!" said she. "No wonder ol' Gally Mander hasn't come home! She's done forgot to take her money with her!"

So off ran the girl with the long leather purse to give back the money to nasty ol' Gally Mander. But when the cow she met asked to be milked, this girl milked it. And when the horse asked to have his back rubbed, this girl rubbed it. And when the tree asked her to pick peaches to ease its sore limbs, this girl picked them all off.

And when ol' Gally Mander came hollerin' down the road,

"Gally Mander, Gally Mander, what could be worse!

That gal's run off with my long leather purse,"
the cow said, "T'ain't seen nobody a-tall." The horse said, "T'aint seen nobody a-tall." And the tree said,

"That gal's got no time to fool with you, honey.

She's gone clear 'round the world with all yer money!"
Nasty ol' Gally Mander hollered and boo-hooed all the way home. There she stayed with nothin' but ash cakes to eat for the rest of her life. Stingy ol' cuss got what she deserved. And the girl sailed off to London, where she lived like a queen.

81

# Possum

Possum up a gum stump,
Cooney in the holler;
Little boy, you shake 'em out,
I'll give you half a dollar.

Possum up a gum stump,
Cooney in the holler,
And a little gal at Pappy's house
As fat as she can waller.

# Jack Runs Off

This here's a story about a boy named Jack. He was a good boy and all, but he didn't like work, and that's a fact. It seems like his head was always lost somewheres up there in the clouds. He would piddle around and nothin' would ever get done.

As more and more chores piled up, what Jack fine-ly got was a good whuppin'. So he left. Right then and there, Jack decided to make do somewheres else besides home.

Off he took, a-walkety-walkin' down the ol' dusty dirt road. Soon he heard, *"Um-mmm-moowh! Um-um-moowh!"* It was one droopy ol' ox, a-whoopin' and a-bellowin' to beat the band.

"Hello," says Jack. "What's the matter with you?"

"Law me!" says the ox. "I'm good fer nothin'. I'm too old to plow. Now I'm gonna get killed off."

"Come run away with me," says Jack. "Let's make do together somewheres else."

So off they took, the ox and Jack, a walkety-walkin' down the ol' dusty dirt road. Soon they heard, *"Haw-hee-haw! Haw-hee-haw!"*

It was one sorrowful-lookin' donkey with his head hangin' between his knobby knees.

"Hello," says Jack. "What's the matter with you?"

"Law me!" says the donkey. "I'm good fer nothin'. I'm too old and weak to haul wood. Now I'm gonna get killed off."

"Come run away with us," says Jack. "Let's make do together somewheres else."

So off they took, the donkey, the ox, and Jack, a-walkety-walkin' down the ol' dusty dirt road. Soon they heard, *"Ow-ow-owooh! Ow-ow-owooh!"*

It was one lonely ol' hound dog, a-settin' and a-frettin'.

"Hello," says Jack. "What's the matter with you?"

"Law me!" says the hound dog. "I'm good fer nothin.' My legs are so limp I cain't hunt coon. I'm gonna get killed off."

"Come run away with us," says Jack. "Let's make do together somewheres else."

So off they took, the hound dog, the donkey, the ox, and Jack, a-walkety-walkin' down the ol' dusty dirt road. Soon they heard, *"Mee-eee-yowl! Mee-eee-yowl!"*

It was one scrawny, pitiful-lookin' squallin' cat.

"Hello," says Jack. "What's the matter with you?"

"Law me!" says the cat. "My teeth are so loose, I cain't catch rats no more. I'm gonna get killed off."

"Come run away with us," says Jack. "Let's make do together somewheres else."

So off they took, the cat, the hound dog, the donkey, the ox, and Jack, a-walkety-walkin' down the ol' dusty dirt road. Soon they heard, *"Arook-arook-aroo! Arook-arook-aroo!"*

It was one stringy-feathered rooster, a-crowin' like it was midnight.

"Hello," says Jack. "What's the matter with you?"

"Law me!" says the rooster. "Company's comin' and I'm gonna be baked in a pie."

"Come run away with us," says Jack. "Let's make do together somewheres else."

So off they took, the rooster, the cat, the hound dog, the donkey, the ox, and Jack, a-walkety-walkin' down the ol' dusty dirt road.

Come nightfall everbody was so tired, they all hitched a ride on the donkey's back. "Looky yonder," says the donkey. "There's an ol' empty house."

"Hello!" called Jack, but nobody answered.

When they had a look inside, their mouths hung open wide.

Why, that house was full to the brim with money, jewels, and enough vittles to last a lifetime.

"If you ask me, robbers live here," says the ol' donkey.

"If it's robbers," says Jack, "then we've got as much right to all this as they do."

"Yes," says the ol' dog. "But if all this belongs to a bunch of robbers, they'll be back."

"And if they'll be back, we better hide," says the ol' cat.

"Matter of fact," says the rooster, "here they come directly."

Quickety-quick, they all hid. Ox in the yard. Donkey on the

porch. Dog behind the door. Cat in the fireplace. And ol' rooster on the roof.

Along came the robbers. One ran ahead to light a fire, so the others could see to get in. When he bent over the fireplace, he saw two cat eyes a-glowin'.

"Looka here," he said, "two coals afire! *Phewt!*" He blew on those coals with all his might.

SCRATCHETY SCRATCH! The cat clawed his cheeks.

YIPES! The robber ran for the door.

CHOMP! The dog bit his leg.

OW! He ran onto the porch.

KAPOW! The donkey kicked him out into the yard.

YIIIIII! The ox caught him with his horns and tossed him into the bushes.

CHUNKA-DUNKA-DEE! And rooster started crowin' right big.

When the other robbers heard the racket, they came a-runnin' . . . and bumped right into the first one, who was flyin' as fast as a bolt of lightnin'.

"Oh, I'm killed," he bawled. "I'm killed for good!"

"Well," said the others. "Don't die without tellin' us what happened back yonder."

"Law me!" said the robber, a-shiverin' and a-shakin'. "That house is plumb full of the meanest, worstest, awfulest men you ever laid your eyes on. One in the fireplace raked me with an awl. One behind the door chopped my leg with a butcher knife. One

on the porch hit me with a plow and knocked me clean off to the yard, where another with a pitchfork threw me over the fence. Then, to top it off, that man up on the roof hollered out, 'Chunk him up here! Chunk him up here!'"

So the robbers ran. They ran and they ran and they ran until they ran plumb out the country.

Now all the riches and good things to eat belong to Jack, the ox, the donkey, the dog, the cat, and the rooster. And to this very day, they are still havin' themselves a grand ol' time!

## Bakin'

There's some that like the fat of the meat,
And some that like the lean,
But they that have no cake to bake
Can keep their kitchens clean.

## Chicken Pie

Chicken pie, made of rye;
A possum was the meat;
Rough enough, and tough enough,
But more'n we all can eat.

## Gray Horse

Edmund had an ol' gray horse.
Its name was Morgan Brown.
Every tooth in Morgan's head
Was fifteen miles around.

## Ticks

As I went down to my ol' field,
I heard a mighty maulin'.
The seed ticks was a-splittin' rails;
The chiggers was a-haulin'.

# Three Foots

Way up yonder on the tippy top of a tall mountain, there once lived three squirrels. The young'un's name was Foot. His ma was called Foot-Foot. And, a course, his pa had to be called Foot-Foot-Foot 'cause he was the biggest.

Now these squirrels weren't right smart in the head. If they'd had a lick of sense, they would've never settled down to live on a bald-faced mountain where nothin' much grows that's good to eat. But sure enough they did, and it wasn't long before Foot, Foot-Foot, and Foot-Foot-Foot got to feelin' mighty hungry.

Right then, Foot told Foot-Foot, "I'm so hungry, I could eat rocks."

Foot-Foot told Foot-Foot-Foot, "Foot-Foot-Foot, your son is so hungry, he's a-gonna eat this whole entire mountain right up."

After thinkin' and thinkin' and thinkin' a good long while, Foot-Foot-Foot said, "Foot-Foot, you and Foot foller me."

Off they'uns went, round and round and all the way down the side of the mountain. 'Course it took forever, which made Foot, Foot-Foot, and Foot-Foot-Foot hungrier than a bunch of half-starved hogs.

Right there at the bottom of the holler was the tangliest ol' giant of a nut tree a-standin' there just so. It held out its arms like it was fixin' to throw out a welcome mat.

Seein' this, Foot, Foot-Foot, and Foot-Foot-Foot could barely contain themselves. Why, with their tails a-twitchin' and their tongues a-danglin', they pretty near had an out-and-out fit of pure anticipation.

"I'm a-gonna start at the bottom and eat all the way up to the top," said Foot.

"I'm a-gonna start at the top and eat all the way down to the bottom," said Foot-Foot-Foot.

"Well, I guess I'll just start in the middle and eat a little ways up and a little ways down and a little ways all around," said Foot-Foot.

And so, they commenced to eat.

Foot at the bottom. *Chew! Chew! Chew!*

Foot-Foot in the middle. *Chaw! Chaw! Chaw!*

And Foot-Foot-Foot at the top. *Chomp! Chomp! Chomp!*

After a while, Foot complained to Foot-Foot. "Foot-Foot, please tell Foot-Foot-Foot my innards hurt."

So Foot-Foot told Foot-Foot-Foot that Foot did not feel so good.

It took time to sink in, but fine-ly, after thinkin' and thinkin' and thinkin' some more, Foot-Foot-Foot told Foot-Foot that Foot had eaten too fast. So Foot-Foot-Foot told Foot-Foot to tell Foot to slow down.

But it was too late. Foot never got Foot-Foot-Foot's message from Foot-Foot because Foot passed out.

Meanwhile, Foot-Foot and Foot-Foot-Foot commenced to eat some more.

After a spell, Foot-Foot didn't feel so well. So Foot-Foot told Foot-Foot-Foot that she was sick, too.

This worried Foot-Foot-Foot. Foot-Foot-Foot got to thinkin' and thinkin' and thinkin' this over for the longest time.

Fine-ly, Foot-Foot-Foot said to Foot-Foot, "Maybe you ate too fast, Foot-Foot. Slow down."

But by the time Foot-Foot-Foot's message got to Foot-Foot, Foot-Foot was lyin' next to Foot—*out cold!*

Just like before, Foot-Foot-Foot ate some more. Pretty soon, Foot-Foot-Foot didn't feel so good either.

So Foot-Foot-Foot called to Foot-Foot and Foot. "Foot-Foot! Foot! Your ol' pa Foot-Foot-Foot's sick, too!"

'Course, Foot-Foot and Foot couldn't hear Foot-Foot-Foot 'cause they were still out cold.

Law, right then and there came the mightiest crash and— BLAM!—down fell Foot-Foot-Foot. Now there they all were— Foot, Foot-Foot, Foot-Foot-Foot *at the foot of the tree!*

That's where they laid—*and that's where they stayed.*

So the moral of this story is . . . always make sure one foot knows what the other foot is doin'.

# Five Little Pigs

This little pig says, "Let's steal some wheat."

This little pig says, "Where'll ye git it at?"

This little pig says, "In master's barn."

This little pig says, "I'll run and tell."

This little pig says, "Quee, quee, quee, can't get over the doorsill."

# Mountain Superstitions

When a rooster crows in at the door
it is a sign that a vistor is coming.

When you see a redbird, you will see
your sweetheart before the day is over.

If your right eye itches, you will cry.
If your left eye itches, you will laugh.

If your ears burn, somebody is saying bad things about you.

Circle around the sun,
will rain none.
Circle around the moon,
will rain soon.

It is bad luck to see the new moon through bushes or the branches of a tree.

Seeing a flock of birds fly past brings good luck.

Feathers and dogs draw lightning. You must keep away from the feather bed during a thunderstorm and put the dog out of the house.

# ol' sam

Ol' Sam Simonses young Sam Simons is
Ol' Sam Simonses son.
And young Sam Simons will be
Ol' Sam Simons when
Ol' Sam Simons is hung.

# Source Notes

The material used in this book has been gathered from a wide number of sources, and, in most cases, many versions exist. The author wishes to thank the following for permission to use source materials:

**One Cold Day**
This is my own retelling of a Louisiana Creole tale translated by Barry Jean Ancelot in his book, *Cajun and Creole Folktales: The French Oral Tradition of South Louisiana*, which was published by Garland Publishing, Inc., New York, in 1994.

**Monkey Stew**
Collected and translated by Alcée Fortier, this Louisiana Creole tale was recorded in the *Memoirs of the American Folklore Society, Volume 2,* and published in 1895 by Houghton Mifflin Company in Boston. A similar version can be found in *Folktales of All Nations*, edited by F. H. Lee, which was published in 1946 by Tudor Publishing Company in New York. Though I've used my own voice to retell the story, the plot remains unchanged.

**Fool John**
This retelling is actually a combination of several stories about the Cajun simpleton known as "Jean Sotte." Cultures all over the world have created countless tales about a fool who gets himself into trouble, then unwittingly finds a way out. My retelling has a new ending, as I did not wish to include any references to beatings or whippings that were mentioned in the originals. Much of the plot is based on the version recorded by Alcée Fortier in 1895 under the title of "Louisiana Folktales," found in the *Memoirs of the American Folklore Society, Volume 2,* Houghton Mifflin, Boston. Other references include Goustav Lanctot's story in his "Collection d'Adelard Lambert," *Journal of American Folklore, Volume 36,* 1923, and in Corinne L. Saucier's book, *Folk Tales from French Louisiana*, Exposition Press, New York, 1962.

**Possum Plays Dead**
I first heard this Caddo tale from a Choctaw woman at a festival in Florida. In her version, it was a bear who tried to imitate the possum. Years later, at a Native American gathering in Pennsylvania, a Cherokee storyteller repeated this same tale, using a fox instead of a bear. Both told me it had come from the Caddo, who passed it along. A written version told by the Sac and Fox is recorded in the *Journal of American Folklore*, volume 14, published in 1901. It may be that the Sac and Fox first heard the story told when the Caddo migrated northward and settled in their territory.

**The Big Dinin'** and **Mister Grumpy Rides the Clouds**
These were among many stories collected by Emma M. Backus in the South at the turn of the century under different titles. "When Brer Frog Give a Big Dining" is from her collection, "Folk-tales from Georgia," in the *Journal of American Folklore, Volume 13,* published in 1900. "When Mr. Terrapin Went Riding on the Clouds" is from "Animal Tales from North Carolina," published by the *Journal of American Folklore, Volume 12,* in 1899.

### The Watermillion Patch

Previously called "Bro' Rabbit an' De Water-millions," this is among many stories in "Negro Tales from Georgia," collected by Mrs. Ethel Holton Leetner and published by the *Journal of American Folklore, Volume 25,* in 1912.

### Ol' Mister Biggety

This rooster fable can be found in "Folklore of the Southern Negroes," by William Owens, for *Lippincotts* magazine, Volume 20, Philadelphia, December, 1877, and is also in Joel Chandler Harris's *Nights with Uncle Remus*, Houghton Mifflin, Boston, 1911.

### How Come Ol' Buzzard Boards

In 1902, Martha Young (1862–1941), who grew up on a plantation in Alabama where her father kept slaves, put together a large collection of bird stories in her book, *Plantation Bird Legends*, published by R. H. Russell Company in 1902. This tale is among those she recorded.

### Nuts! Nuts! Nuts!

Originally called "Rabbit Outwits Panther," this is my own retelling of an old Creek tale first recorded by Frank G. Speck in his detailed study, "The Creek Indians of Taskigi Town," published by the *American Anthropological Society Memoirs 2:2,* in 1907. The Creek once lived all over the Deep South, particularly in what is now Georgia.

### Ol' Gally Mander

Previous versions of this silly tale based on the old English folktale "The Old Witch" are much longer than mine. I omitted some of the repetition, thus greatly condensing the last part of the story. My retelling includes rhymed refrains that are not part of other versions in print. My source can be found in "Mountain White Folk-lore: Tales from the Southern Blue Ridge," collected in 1923 by Isabel Gordon Carter, *Journal of American Folklore, Volume 25,* 1925.

### Jack Runs Off

This is a retelling of just one of many Jack tales narrated by Maud Long and recorded at the Library of Congress in 1947. Originally called "Jack and the Robbers," it is the Appalachian version of "The Bremen Town Musicians," an old German tale. Richard Chase also put together a collection, "The Jack Tales," which were told to him by R. M. Ward and other descendants of Council Harmon (1803-1896) from Beech Mountain, North Carolina. His collection was published by Houghton Mifflin Company in Boston in 1943.

### Three Foots

I first heard this story way back when I was a counselor at a summer camp in the Tennessee Mountains. It was one of those favorites told by the campfire, but the camp version was a lot more gory than the one retold here. I had nearly forgotten about it until my good friend Lenape Chief Bill "Whip-poor-will" Thompson told it again at a gathering in Pennsylvania. His version, though, is about wooly mammoths—not squirrels! And, it has a different ending. Just recently on a train headed South, I dined with a young couple who live just outside Boone, North Carolina. Sure enough, they told me this same old story all over again. I decided a retelling would be fun to do for this collection.

*Tails, I Had a Little Dog, Bat, The Watermelon, The Old Hen Cackled, The Rooster, The Grasshopper,* and *Did You Feed My Cow?* were collected by Thomas Talley in his book, *Negro Folk Rhymes,* published in 1922 by Kennikat Press, New York. *The Squirrel, Little Horsies, Dreamland,* and *The Goat* are included in *In the Nursery,* Volume 1, edited by Olive Beaupré Miller, published by The Book House for Children, Chicago, in 1920. *Ol' Man Dan, Ticks, Possum, Five Little Pigs, Bakin', Chicken Pie,* and *Ol' Sam* are recorded in "The Spirit of the Mountains," a collection from Appalachia by Emma Miles, published by James Pott & Company in 1905. *What You Got There?* is in a collection titled "Notes on Folkore of Guilford County, North Carolina," by Elsie Clews Parsons, *Journal of American Folklore, Volume 26,* 1913. An English version can be found in the *Oxford Nursery Rhyme Book* as "What's in There." *Gray Horse* was recorded in the East Tennessee Mountains in 1912 and can be found in the *Journal of American Folklore, Volume 26. Nobody Likes Me* is in the collection by E. C. Perrow, "Songs and Rhymes from the South," *Journal of American Folklore, Volume 28,* 1915. *Gumbo* is in the Langston Hughes collection, *The Book of Negro Folklore,* Dodd, Mead, New York, 1958. *The Egg, The Bee,* and *We Hunted and We Hollered* are in *The Encyclopedia of Black Folklore and Humor,* compiled and edited by Henry D. Spalding, Jonathan David Publishers, 1972, reprinted in 1990. *We Hunted and We Hollered* is based on the old English rhyme "Three Men Went a-Hunting."

Most of the riddles were recorded by Elsie Clews Parsons for the *Journal of American Folklore* from various parts of the South, including Guilford County, North Carolina, and the Sea Islands, South Carolina, published between 1917 and 1922. Many of the superstitions and sayings in *With a Whoop and a Holler* were contributed by my Southern friends and relatives. Other sources include Henry C. Davis's "Negro Folklore in South Carolina," *Journal of American Folklore, Volume 27,* 1914; Parker Haywood's "Folklore of the North Carolina Mountaineers," *Journal of American Folklore, Volume 20,* 1907; Lafcadio Hearn's *Gombo Zhebes: Little Dictionary of Creole Proverbs,* Will H. Coleman, New York, 1885; Roland Steiner's "Superstitions from Central Georgia," and H. M. Wiltse's "Some Mountain Superstitions of the South," both in the *Journal of American Folklore, Volume 12,* 1899.

# Other Useful Sources

Abrahams, Rogers. *African American Folktales: Stories from Black Traditions to the New World.* New York: Pantheon Books, 1985.

Atchity, Kenneth Aguillard. *Cajun Household Wisdom.* Connecticut: Longmeadow Publishing, 1995.

Botkin, B. A. *A Treasury of Southern Folklore.* New York: Crown Publishers, 1949.

Bronsard, James F. *Louisiana Creole Dialect.* Baton Rouge, LA: Louisiana State University, 1942.

*The Frank C. Brown Collection of North Carolina Folklore.* Durham, NC: Duke University Press, 1952.

Buel, James W. *Legends of the Ozarks.* St. Louis: W. S. Bryan, 1880.

Cable, George W. *The Creoles of Louisiana.* New York: Charles Scribner, 1884.

Carmer, Carl. *Stars Fell on Alabama.* New York: Farrar & Rinehart, 1934.

Chase, Richard. *Grandfather Tales.* Boston: Houghton Mifflin, 1948.

Christensen, Mrs. H.M.H. *African American Folklore Told Around Cabin Fires on the SeaIsland of South Carolina.* Boston: J. G. Cupples, 1892.

Courlander, Harold. *A Treasury of African American Folklore.* New York: Crown, 1976.

Davidson, Levette J. *A Guide to American Folklore.* New York: Greenwood Press, 1951.

Dorsen, Richard. *Negro Folktales.* Bloomington, IN: University of Indiana Press, 1958.

Faulkner, William. *The Days When Animals Talked: Black American Folktales.* Chicago: Follett, 1977.

Gonzales, Ambrose. *The Black Border: Gullah Stories of the Carolina Coast.* Columbus, SC: The State Co., 1922.

Goss, Linda and Clay. *Jump Up and Say: A Collection of Black Storytelling.* New York: Simon and Schuster, 1995.

Harris, Joel Chandler. *Uncle Remus: His Songs and His Sayings.* Boston: Houghton Mifflin, 1915.

Hudson, Arthur Palmer. *Humor of the Old Deep South.* New York: Macmillan, 1936.

Hurston, Zora Neal. *Mules and Men.* Philadelphia: J. B. Lippincott, 1935.

Jacobs, Joseph. *English Fairy Tales.* (1890; reprint, New York: G. P. Putnam & Sons, 1911.)

Jones, Charles Colcock. *Negro Myths from the Georgia Coast.* Boston: Houghton Mifflin, 1888.

Kane, Harnett T. *The Bayous of Louisiana.* New York: The Hampton Publishing Company, 1944.

MacKaye, Percy. *Tall Tales of the Kentucky Mountains.* New York: George H. Doran, 1926.

Moore, John Trotwood. *Songs and Stories from Tennessee.* Chicago: J. C. Bauer, 1897.

Reneaux, J. J. *Cajun Folktales.* Little Rock, AR: August House, 1992.

Saxon, Lyle. *Gumbo Ya Ya.* Boston: Houghton Mifflin, 1945.